W9-BBZ-332

THE RIDDLE HORSE

Mark Summers

Creative ✦ Editions

Text and illustrations copyright © 2016 by Mark Summers   Edited by Kate Riggs   Designed by Rita Marshall   Published in 2016 by Creative Editions   P.O. Box 227, Mankato, MN 56002 USA

Creative Editions is an imprint of The Creative Company   www.thecreativecompany.us   All rights reserved. No part of the contents of this book may be reproduced by any means without the written permission of the publisher.   Printed in China   Library of Congress Cataloging-in-Publication Data   Name: Summers, Mark.   Title: The Riddle Horse / by Mark Summers.

Summary: In this gentle riddle of a tale, a well-loved horse recounts its adventures and various riders throughout the long years of its curiously restricted yet imaginatively rich life.

Identifiers: LCCN 2015047479 / ISBN 978-1-56846-291-2   Subjects: CYAC: Merry-go-round horses—Fiction. / Riddles—Fiction.   Classification: PZ7.1.S854 Ri 2016 / [E]—dc23

First edition 9 8 7 6 5 4 3 2 1

Every day, I stand next to a mirror,
but I have never seen myself in it.
The eyes of my riders are my mirrors.
Their smiles say I am the most beautiful horse
they have ever seen.

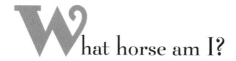

What horse am I?

When I was young,
I charged up San Juan Hill
with Teddy Roosevelt
on my back.

When I was a little older,
I carried cowboys and cowgirls along dusty trails.

Some riders called themselves
John Wayne and Tom Mix or
Zorro and Dale Evans.

What horse am I?

I have carried

many a knight in shining armor

And many damsels fleeing dragons.

I have won the Derby
and medaled in every Olympics.
Always.

What horse am I?

I have galloped thousands of miles
through jungles and deserts
and over snow-capped mountains.

Yet I have never been
more than 30 feet from where
I started.

I have chased a swan for almost 100 years—
and still have not caught it.

Then again, a lion has been chasing me
for just as long, and I always escape.

What horse am I?

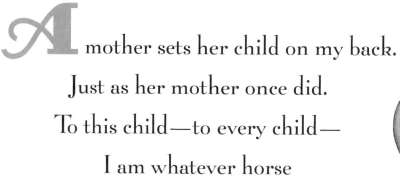

A mother sets her child on my back.
Just as her mother once did.
To this child—to every child—
I am whatever horse
she can imagine.

For my name is "Carousel."